Merry Christmas to 1...

ad key

MW00999133

GoD and DoG

Wendy Francisco

The whole story of GoD and DoG is remarkable. Forty days after the animated video was posted on YouTube, my family and friends and I were astounded to see that it had received over a million views. The video then began to circulate all over the internet with millions of views. Letters poured in by email and for months we tearfully read the most amazing stories of how the song had affected people. It became obvious that we should publish it in book form.

GoD and DoG

Copyright © 2010 by Wendy Francisco

Center Street
Hachette Book Group
237 Park Avenue
New York, NY 10017

www.centerstreet.com

Illustrations by Wendy Francisco
www.WendyFranciso.com

Cover and interior design by Koechel Peterson & Associates, Minneapolis, MN

Center Street is a division of Hachette Book Group, Inc.
The Center Street name and logo are trademarks of Hachette Book Group, Inc.

Printed in the United States of America

First Edition: September 2010
10 9 8 7 6 5 4 3 2 1

LCCN: 2010932061
ISBN 978-1-59995-379-3

There is a wonderful group of people behind this book, all of whom were excited to be a part of telling this story to you.

Thank you to my husband, Don, who is my greatest encourager and the first to hear all my songs. Thank you to my canine soulmate, Caspian, the inspiration for the video.

My deepest thanks to Sarah Jane Freymann, my agent, for many hours of guidance and dedicated work; and to Dana Long for experienced creative direction. What a privilege it is to work with you both. Thank you to Stacey O'Brien for your steadfast encouragement, and congratulations on your New York Times bestselling book, *Wesley the Owl*. I learned all about books by working with you. What an amazing adventure it has been. Thank you to Harry Helm and Center Street Publishing. I will never forget your email containing photographs of every dog owned by your entire staff! Thank you to Koechel Peterson and Associates in Minneapolis. You contributed your professional and creative brilliance to the book and made it beautiful. Thank you to dear friend Mike Banta for helping me do the sheet music.

GoD and DoG is dedicated to my mother, Cathlene Hofheimer, one of the most creative people I have ever met.

And finally, thank you God for filling the earth with authentic thinking loving beings who reflect who you are. We flourish when we are loved, animals flourish when they are loved.

You are the God of love, and you've woven that message into the fabric of creation. You love each of us far more than we can imagine. I hope and pray that after people read GoD and DoG, they will look up, and down, in a new way.

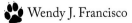 Wendy J. Francisco

I *look* up

I look down

and see my
DoG

Simple spelling...

G·O·D

Same word *backwards,*

D·O·G

They
would
stay
with
me
all
day.

I'm the one

Both **LOVE** me...

And $Dance$ at my
return with **glee**.

who

walks

away.

But both of them

just wait

for me...

No *matter* what.

Divine God

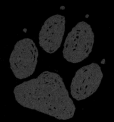
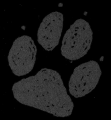

...and **canine mutt**

I take it hard

each time I fail.

but

GoD

forgives

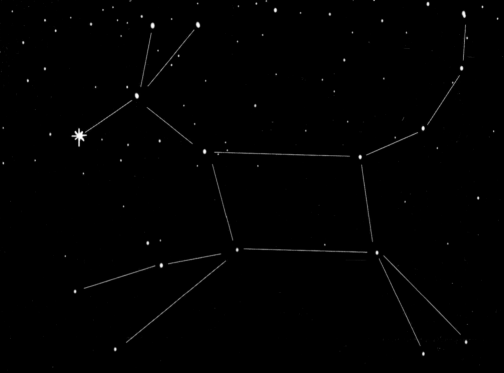

and *made* the DoG

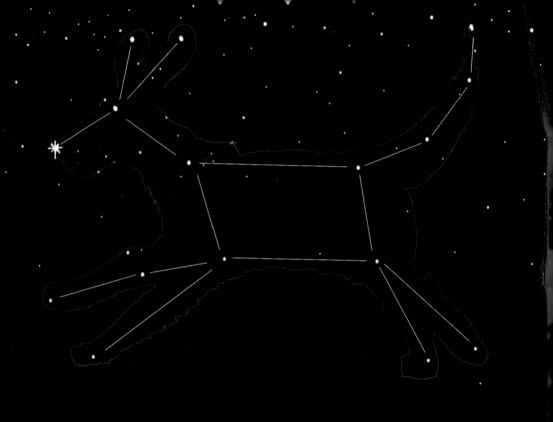

DoG reflects

a *part* of GoD

I've

seen

LOVE

from

both

sides

now

It's EveRywhEre

Amen

🐾 Bow Wow 🐾

and I see
GoD

I look down

and see my
DoG

And in my

human frailty...

I can't match

their *love* for me

GoD and DoG

Words and Music by
WENDY FRANCISCO

Freely!

1. I look up and I see God I look down and see my dog
2. Both love me no mat-ter what Di-vine God and ca-nine mutt I
3. I look up and I see God I look down and see my dog And

Sim - ple spel - ling G O D Same word back-wards D O G
take it hard each time I fail But God for-gives, dog wags his tail
in my hu-man fra - il - ty

They would stay with me all day I'm the one who walks a - way But
God thought up and made the dog Dog re - flects a part of God

both of them just wait for me and dance at my re - turn with glee
I've seen love from both sides now It's ev' - ry - where, A - men, bow - wow

Coda

I can't match their love for me

Caspian,
My Big White Dog
Faithful though
The snow + fog
Guards the ranch
With his great bark
Leads me when
The sky gets dark

-Deleted Verse-